MY NAME IS

AND I AM A BIG BROTHER!

Hello! My name is **Rex**.
I heard you are a
big brother. Me too!
That is **roar-some**!

Hi! We are Rex's friends.
Come **explore** the island with us and
meet the other **big brother** dinos!
Are you ready?
Let's go!

BABY DINO IS ALMOST HERE!

The **Brontosaurus** family is waiting for **Baby Dino** to hatch. **Big Brother** is patiently waiting to meet his new little brother or sister!

BIG BROTHER IS SO EXCITED!

Can you color the dinosaur family and egg?

MOMMY DINO NEEDS YOUR HELP

Can you help Mommy Dino back to the nest? Big Brother is watching over the nest and it looks like the eggs are going to hatch soon! Which path should she take?

MOMMY AND EGG COLOR MATCHING

Can you color match the mommy dinosaurs and eggs?

The wait is over! One of the **baby dinos** has hatched! Let's go meet the newest dino on the island!

WELCOME TO THE WORLD BABY DINO!

Everyone is excited to meet Baby Dino. It is a very special day!

BIG BROTHER MATCHING

Can you find all the matching big brother dinosaurs?

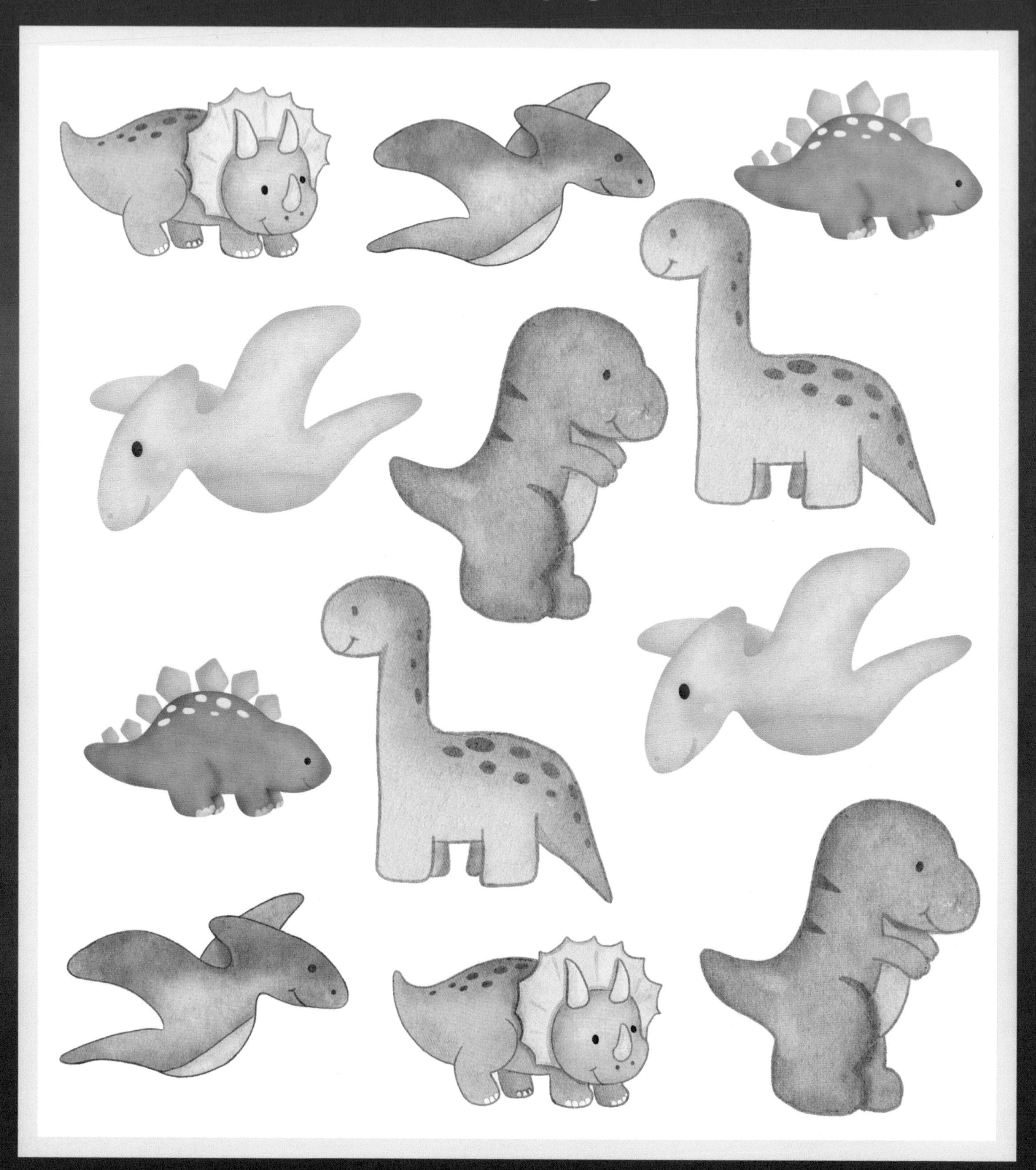

LOOK WHO IS THE BIGGEST NOW!

Big Brother is excited to be the biggest. He used to be small like Baby Dino, but now he is the big brother!

At first, **baby dinos** need a lot of attention and care. They sleep a lot and sometimes they cry a lot, too! Usually, when they cry, they are just sleepy or hungry.
I like **helping** mommy take care of Baby Dino. She gives me special **big brother jobs**!

BIG BROTHER IS A BIG HELPER!

Big Brother helps cheer up Baby Dino by showing Baby Dino one of his favorite toys.

DADDY AND BROTHER DINO NEED YOUR HELP

Can you help Daddy Dino and Big Brother Dino back home?
Which path should they take?

BIG BROTHER IS A GOOD STORYTELLER!

Big Brother is telling Baby Dino one of his favorite bedtime stories!

BIG BROTHER NEEDS YOUR HELP

Can you help Brother Dino climb down the hill? If you get lost, follow the dino tracks to the bottom of the hill.

BIG BROTHER
COLOR BY NUMBER

Use the color key to color this happy big brother!

1

2

3

4

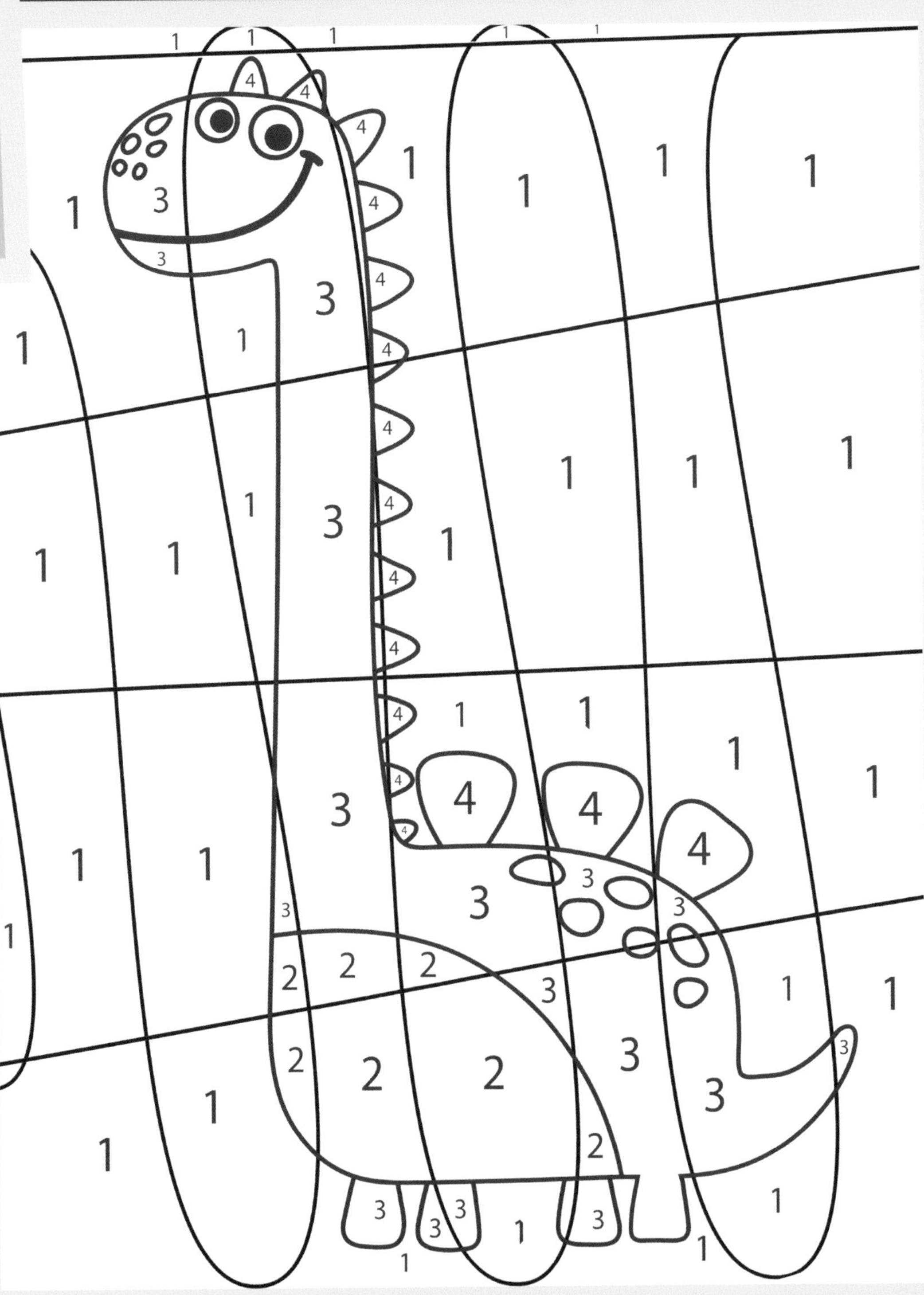

FINISH THE PICTURE

Can you add spikes to Baby Stegosaurus and finish coloring the page?

BIG LAUGHS AND BIG SMILES!

Big Brother T-Rex likes to make Baby T-Rex smile and laugh with his funny stories and songs!

HOW MANY BABY DINOS CAN YOU COUNT?

1

2

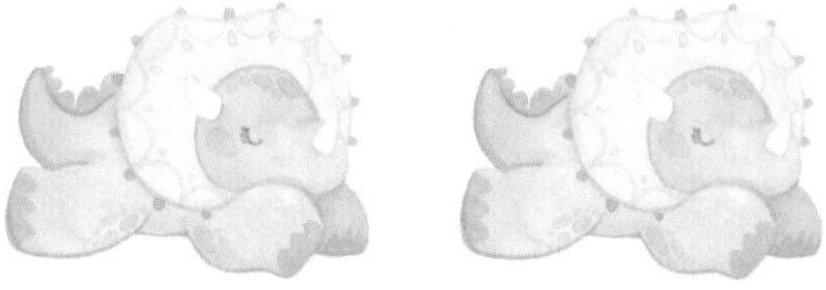

3

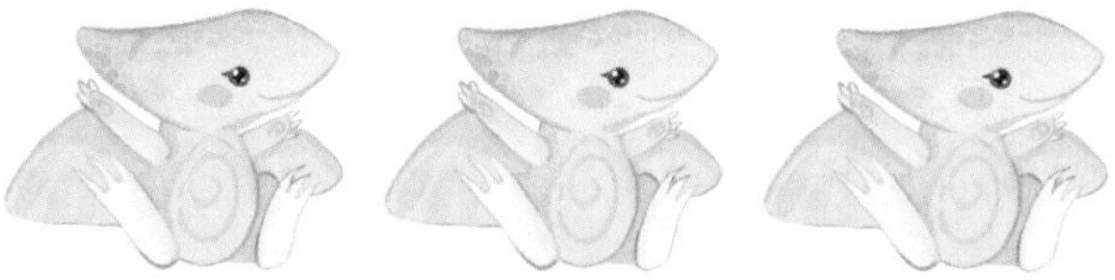

4

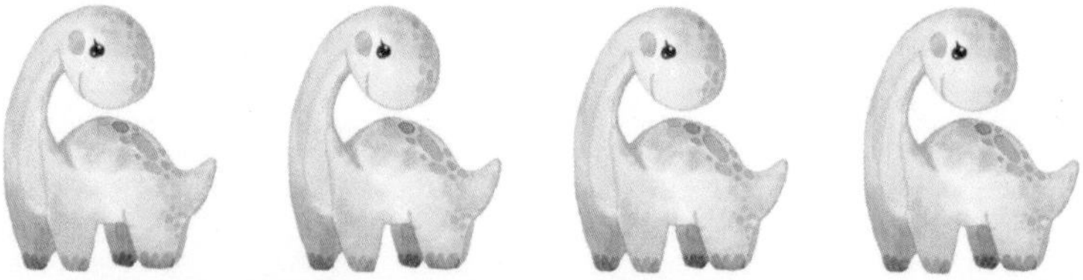

5

6

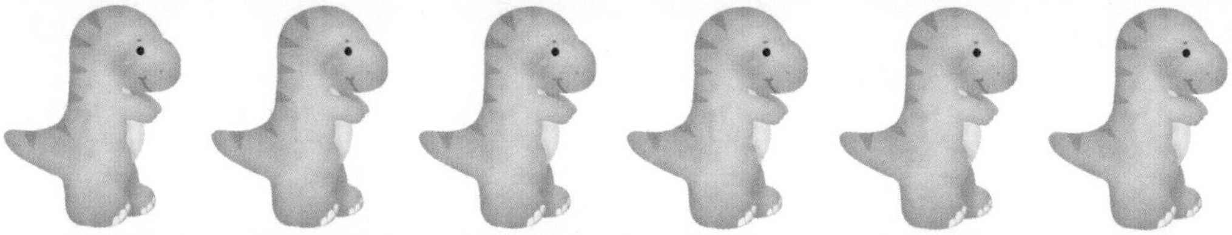

BIG BROTHER RIDES ARE THE BEST!

Baby Dino is still learning to walk. In the meantime, Baby Dino loves rides from Big Brother!

WHO IS THEIR BIG BROTHER?

Can you match the baby dinos on the left to their big brother on the right?

BIG BROTHER IS SO MUCH FUN!

Big Brother is a fun slide for Baby Dino!

The **baby dinos** are quickly growing up! As they get bigger, the big brother dinos can **teach** them a lot of new things!
What can you **teach** your baby brother or sister as they grow up?

BIG BROTHER IS A GOOD TEACHER!

Big Brother Plesiosaur is teaching Little Plesiosaur how to swim!

FUN AT THE PARK

The big brother dinos and little dinos are having fun at the park.
Can you find all of them? Can you also find the volcano, bone, and eggs?

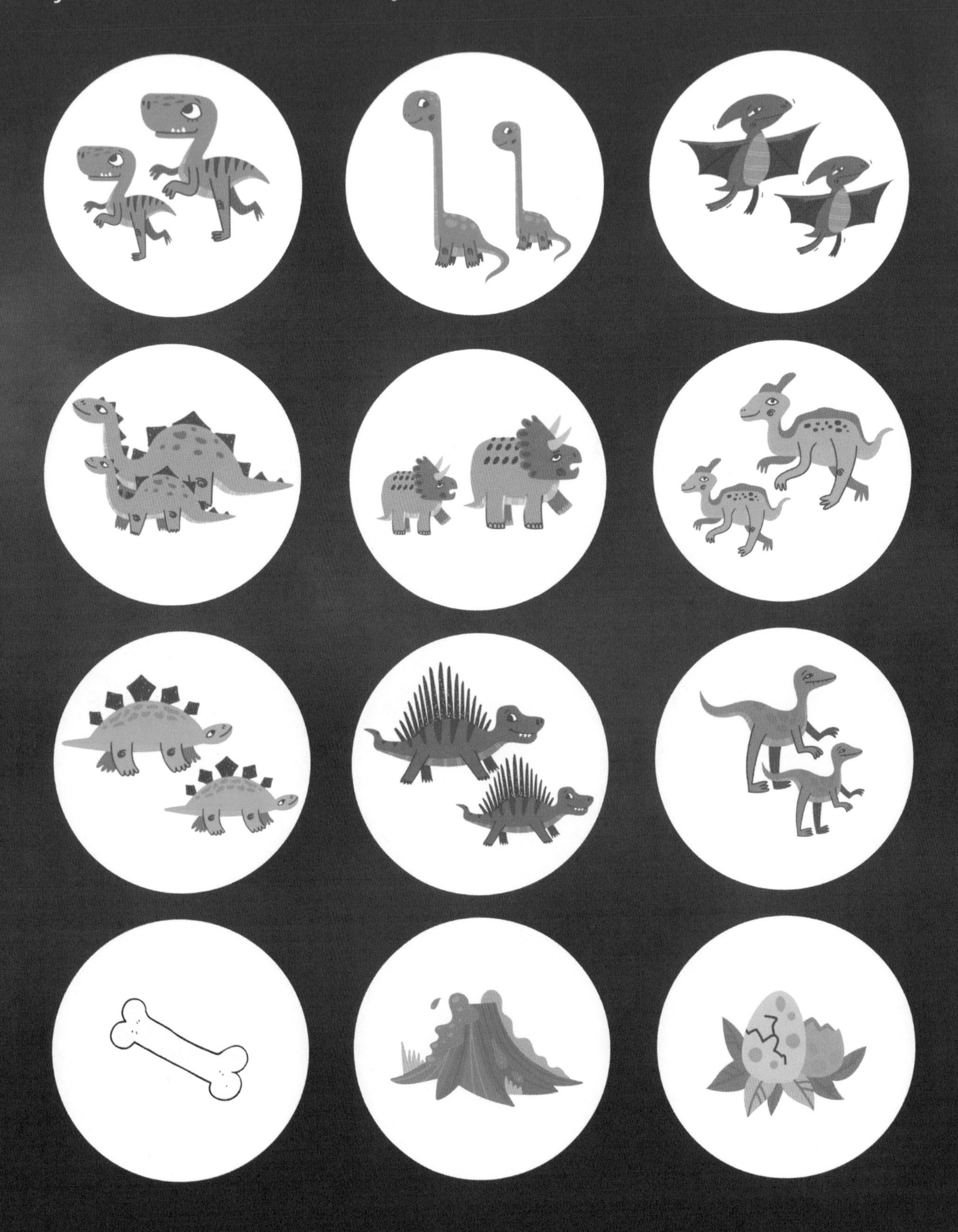

DINOPARK

LOOK WHO IS LEARNING TO FLY!

Big Brother Pterodactyl is teaching Little Pterodactyl how to fly!

PLAYING GAMES WITH BIG BROTHER!

Big Brother is teaching Little Dino how to play ball!

MATCH THE SHADOWS

Can you match the dinosaurs on the left to their shadows on the right?

WHO IS HIDING BEHIND THE TREE?

Big Brother and Little Dino are playing hide and seek!

HELP BIG BROTHER THROUGH THE MAZE

Can you help Big Brother and Little Dino find Mommy Dino?
If you need help, just look for Mommy Dino's tracks.

FINISH THE PICTURE

Can you add a sail to Little Dimetrodon like Big Brother's and finish coloring the page?

Baby dinos are too little to play when they first hatch. As they grow up, though, they can **play** more and more.
Little Dino and I love playing games together. Little Dino and I have become **best friends!**

FLYING TOGETHER IS SO MUCH FUN!

With Big Brother's help, Little Pterodactyl is now flying!

WHAT IS DIFFERENT?

Can you find 10 differences between the two pictures?

WHAT IS THE SAME?

What is the same in the two pictures?

BIG BROTHER IS ROAR-SOME!

Little Triceratops wants to be just like Big Brother Triceratops!

BEING A BIG BROTHER IS THE BEST!

Can you draw a picture of you with your brother or sister?

I hope you had fun with all the **big brother dinosaurs**! You're going to be a **dino-mite big brother**!

Book Design By Zady Rose
Illustrations by Various Artists

Published by Collected Joys
www.collectedjoys.com

First Edition: October 2021
Second Edition: March 2022

Printed in Great Britain
by Amazon

BIG BROTHERS ARE ROAR-SOME!

Explore the anticipation, excitement, and role of being a big brother through fun stories, coloring pages, mazes, spot the differences, and more!

BY ZADY ROSE

PUBLISHED BY COLLECTED JOYS | WWW.COLLECTEDJOYS.COM

ISBN 9798483850380
9 798483 850380